In celebration of
Korea's 70th year of independence
Singapore's 50th year of independence and
40 years of diplomatic relations between the two countries

# 싱가포르 꽃이 들려준 한국 詩

Singapore's flowers whisper Korean poems

**펴 낸 날** 2015년 8월 3일

**지 은 이**   금혜정
**펴 낸 이**   최지숙
**편집주간**   이기성
**편집팀장**   이윤숙
**기획편집**   이호형
**표지디자인**  이호형
**책임마케팅**  임경수
**펴 낸 곳**   도서출판 생각나눔
**출판등록**   제 2008-000008호
**주    소**   서울 마포구 동교로 18길 41, 한경빌딩 2층
**전    화**   02-325-5100
**팩    스**   02-325-5101
**홈페이지**   www.생각나눔.kr
**이 메 일**   webmaster@think-book.com

• 책값은 표지 뒷면에 표기되어 있습니다.
  ISBN 978-89-6489-413-2   03810

• 이 도서의 국립중앙도서관 출판 시 도서목록(CIP)은 서지정보유통지원시스템 홈페이지
  (http://seoji.nl.go.kr)와 국가자료공동목록시스템(http://www.nl.go.kr/kolisnet)에서
  이용하실 수 있습니다(CIP제어번호: CIP2015020247).

싱가포르 꽃이 들려준 한국 詩
Singapore's flowers whisper Korean poems

들어가는 글

  나는 한국인이지만 싱가포르에서 보낸 세월이 거의 십 년에 접어든
다. 열대 꽃을 카메라에 담을 때 마다 싱가포르가 친숙해졌고 세상의
씨앗인 가정의 소중함을 꽃들은 시로 들려 주었다. 꽃 사진에는 독자들
에게 도움이 되고자 식물학적 분류에 의한 학명과 과명을 기재하였다.

  올해 한국은 독립 70주년 그리고 싱가포르는 건국 50주년을 맞았다.
꽃들도 축하를 해주듯 두 나라의 미래가 함께 활짝 피기를 바란다.

2015년 적도에서

빨래를 개며 <sup>part</sup>2<sub>부</sub> Folding laundry

마늘, 꽃이 되다 <sup>part</sup>3<sub>부</sub> Garlic becomes a flower

# 사람소리 part 4 부 Human sounds

녹차 <sup>part</sup>**1**<sub>부</sub> Green tea

Quisqualis indica
Family Name:Combretaceae

# 밥 꽃

이른 아침 꽃 송이는
눈으로 먹는 밥이요

점심 나절 고봉밥은
입으로 보는 꽃이요

해질녘
우리 어머닌
밥 하시는 꽃이다

-2013년 3월 한나프레스-

# Food flower

Early morning flower in blossom
is food for the eyes

Lunchtime bowl of rice aplenty
is a flower for the mouth

Twilight
dear mother
is a flower cooking food

Calotropis gigantea
Family Name:Asclepiadaceae

빨래

Tibouchina urvilleana
Family Name:Melastomataceae

나는 당신이 벗어 놓은
하루의 껍데기입니다
꼭 맞는 신발 안에서 종일
당신과 포옹한 양말입니다
점심 때 흘린 당신의 짠 국물 한 마디가 슬퍼서
깊이 스며든 바짓가랑이의 마음 한 쪽
속이 뒤집힌 채 멍할 때
나보다 오래 산 흰 구름이 지나가며
오늘과 오늘은
강물보다 빨리 흐르는 세월이라 합니다
내일과 내일은
구름인 듯 멀리 떠 있다가도
어느새 떨어져 버리는 빗방울이라 합니다
집으로 돌아오는 어깨에
지친 노을이 물든 당신을 보며
넉넉한 물로 내 전부를 흠뻑 적시고
여기저기 때 묻은 생각도 두어 번 헹구고 나면
소매로 닦았던 당신의 땀방울까지
비 그친 아침처럼 깨끗해지기를
그리고 나는 내일 다시 동행하는
당신의 옷이 될 수 있기를

-제14회 재외동포문학상 수상작-

# Laundry

I am the daily

skin you have shed

the socks that embraced you

in your tight shoes all day

The salty soup your words dripped at lunch

saddens me like a stain on your trousers

As I lay vacantly inside out

white clouds who lived longer than I pass by

saying today and today

are time flowing faster than a river

saying tomorrow and tomorrow

are raindrops that suddenly fall

after floating aloof like a cloud

As I watch your sunset-drenched

shoulders coming home

how I wish to soak myself abundantly with water

to rinse out and again the soiled thoughts all over

so even the sweat wiped off on your sleeves

becomes clean like a morning after the rain

so I can become your clothes again

that walk with you tomorrow

Allamanda blanchetii
Family Name:Apocynaceae

Spathoglottis Phong Chi
Family Name:Orchidaceae

# 녹차

그대가 가슴 속에
끓어 오른 찻물 담아

뜨거운 입김으로
마른 내 잎에 쏟아지면

바스락
소리도 없이
그대에게 녹아 든다

# Green tea

As you take the water
boiled with your heart

And spill it in a heated sigh
onto my withering leaves

Without
a crackle
I melt onto you

Duranta erecta
Family Name:Verbenaceae

Musa acuminata var.
Family Name:Musaceae

# 바나나 꽃

넙적한 잎새 아래
바나나가 맺혀있다

꽃 피고 지는 자리에
태어나는 열매들

피었던 내 꽃도 지니
아이들이 여문다

# Banana flower

Bananas hang
under wide leaves

Fruits that rise
where flowers bloom and fall

As my blooming flowers fall
my children grow

Musa acuminata var.
Family Name:Musaceae

# 밥그릇

Allamanda cathartica
Family Name:Apocynaceae

며칠

식은 밥을 담아 보니

그 밥으로는 내 가슴 한 구석도 데울 수 없어

끓는 밥솥 앞에서 빈 그릇으로 기다립니다

몇 해

설익은 밥을 담아 보니

그 밥으로는 배고픈 자의 마음 하나 익힐 수 없어

뜸 드는 밥솥 앞에서 빈 그릇으로 기다립니다

진정 당신을 향해

알알이 품은 쌀의 꿈을 담아

하얗고 고슬고슬하게 미소 지으며

뜨거운 고봉밥으로 대접해 드리는 일

밥이 시가 되고 노래가 되는 수고는

끈끈하고도 구수하여 여전히

빈 채로 기다릴 수 있습니다

이제 내 속이 잘 익은 밥으로 가득 차면

그 때 내 사랑 한 그릇 호호 불어 드신 후

눈도 귀도 즐거이 당신의 한 나절쯤은

든든하고 행복하시길

그저 바랄 뿐입니다

-2012년 한나프레스 신춘문예 당선작-

# Rice bowl

After a few days

of serving cold rice

I see such rice won't even warm a nook of my heart

so I stand waiting as an empty bowl as the rice cooker boils

After a few years

of serving half-cooked rice

I see such rice cannot even know the pain of the hungry

so I stand waiting as an empty bowl as the rice cooker simmers

To truly serve you

with all the dreams of tiny grains

in a white and ripe smile

a hot full bowl of rice

Laboring rice into a poem and a song

is so sticky and sweet that

I do not mind waiting empty

Now my only wish

when I am filled with well-cooked rice

may you blow the steam off a hot bowl of my love

to spend the short day with pleased eyes and ears

happy and content

Cuphea hyssopifolia
Family Name:Lythraceae

Calliandra emarginata
Family Name:Leguminosae

# 설거지

당신의 그릇에 말라 붙은 밥풀은
억센 수세미로도 달랠 수 없는 고집이라
따뜻한 물로 안아야 굳은 마음 푸신다

# Washing dishes

Dried-up bits of rice
clinging to your bowl
Even the toughest sponge
cannot soothe the stubbornness
Only with warm water's embrace
do you open your callous heart

Beallara Pacific Pastel 'Mauna Loa'
Family Name:Orchidaceae

Wrightia religiosa
Family Name:Apocynaceae

# 행복

보일 듯 말 듯한
밤 하늘의 별들과

물결을 만들지 않고
흐르는 강물과

있는 듯 없는 듯 피는
저 꽃들이 행복해

# Happiness

Stars in the sky
faintly in view

Flow of the river
that makes no ripple

And silent bloom of flowers
all is happiness

Rondeletia leucophylla
Family Name:Rubiaceae

Etlingera elatior
Family Name:Zingiberaceae

# 부등 깃이 따스해

고향 가는 하늘 길 구름보다 들떠서
가만히 기다려도 가슴 속은 파닥파닥
나는야 둥지로 가는 겨울새 한 마리

날아도 날아도 캄캄한 하늘 길에
저 많은 등불을 켜놓은 별들 따라
빛들의 속도로 날면 얼마나 좋을까

날마다 기다리신 어머니 그리느라
밤 새워 날아도 고단한 줄 모르네
둥지로 날아 드는 일 부등 깃이 따스해

먼동이 트는구나 겨울새 날개 접고
흰 눈이 소복이 쌓인 옛 풍경 속으로
사뿐히 내려앉아 어머니 품에 안기리

# My pinfeathers are warm

Flying back home I'm more excited than a cloud
Even as I silently wait my heart wildly flaps
I am a winter bird returning to the nest

In the dark sky path of endless flight
how I wish to fly at the speed of light
along the myriad lamplights kindled by the stars

Longing for my mother who has waited every day
I do not get tired even as I fly all night
Flying back to my nest makes my pinfeathers warm

There comes the dawn; the winter bird will fold its wings
And in the familiar landscape softly covered with white snow
Lightly will it land into her mother's embrace

Leea rubra
Family Name:Leeaceae

Arachnis Maggie Oei
Family Name:Orchidaceae

# 절구

일상을 투덜대며
빨는 일이 지루한 날

우묵한 내 안으로
절굿공이 내려친다

입방아 잘못 찧어서
눈에 튀는 마늘 쪽

# Mortar

A boring day of pounding
my everyday complaints

I strike down the pestle
into my hollow entrails

A piece of garlic flies into my eye
struck by my flippant lips

Combretum comosum
Family Name:Combretaceae

Pseuderanthemum 'Pink'
Family Name:Acanthaceae

# 자전거 나무

나무는 나무인 척 저렇게 서 있어도
둥치 안의 두 발로 서 있는 자전거
나무도 갓난쟁이 땐 얼마나 위태로웠나

가난한 몸매에 쌍 떡잎 하나 머리에 이고
살아남는 일조차 얼마나 무거웠나
파르르 실바람에도 넘어지길 수 차례

젊어서 씽씽 겁 없이 달릴 때는
머리에 돋은 이파리 다 떨어져도 신났네
어느새 어른이 되어 굵직해진 나무 줄기

바지런히 달려 온 자전거 한 그루는
이제 앞이 아니라 위로 달리는 자전거
연마한 세월의 바퀴 멈춰도 넘어지지 않네

# Bicycle tree

Though the tree stands acting like a tree
it is only a bicycle standing with its trunk of two feet
How wobbly was the tree in its newborn days

Its impoverished body with two seed leaves on its head
what a burden it was just to stay alive
Several times did it fall in the slightest vibrating breeze

In its youth as it boldly raced like the wind
it was so proud even as all leaves on its head fell off
In no time an adult, its trunk is already thick

This tree of a bicycle that so tirelessly ran
now runs not forward but upwards
age-polished wheels won't fall even when it stops

Melastoma malabathricum
Family Name:Melastomataceae

Episcia cupreata 'Frosty'
Family Name:Gesneriaceae

# 꽃 단추

어머니의 스웨터에 피어있던 꽃 단추
단추 한 줄로 마음을 여닫으며
꽃가루 뿌리시듯 늘 하시던 잔소리

아버지 천국 가신 날 툭 - 떨어졌네
싱싱한 그 목소리 찬 울음에 시들었네
어쩌나 어머니의 꽃 단추 한 다발

# Flower button

Flower button that blossomed on mother's sweater
Line of buttons that opened and closed her heart
Spilling like flower dust her familiar nagging

Did it fall - tap - on the day father left for heaven
Did her fresh voice wither under cold tears
Alas, mother's bunch of flower buttons

Pseuderanthemum laxiflorum
Family Name:Acanthaceae

Ruellia brittoniana
Family Name:Acanthaceae

# 거기

거기 그렇게 낙엽 지는 가을이라는데
여기 이렇게 세월 모르는 여름입니다
어제도
소낙비에
마음 젖은 꽃잎들

거기 그렇게 눈꽃 피는 겨울이라는데
여기 이렇게 그리움 짙푸른 여름입니다
오늘도
해가 지면
마음도 지는 꽃잎들

# There

There it is autumn full of falling leaves
Yet here it is timeless summer
Yesterday
Under the squall
Flowers were soaked with sadness too

There it is winter of flowering snow
Yet here it is summer green of yearning
Today
As the sun set
Flowers set of longing too

Catharanthus roseus
Family Name：Apocynaceae

빨래를 개며  Folding laundry

Plumeria rubra cultivars
Family Name:Apocynaceae

# 흰 꽃이 피는 나무

나무가 가지 마다 부케를 들고 서서
그늘진 연인들 오래 오래 사랑하라고
꽃 향기 그윽한 얘기 밤을 새워 피운다

# Tree blossoming with white flowers

The tree holds bouquets on every little branch
So the lovers' love in its shadows may live on and on
Growing stories of flowery scent all through the night

Pleiocarpa mutica
Family Name:Apocynaceae

Neonauclea purpurea
Family Name:Rubiaceae

# 이웃의 향기

앞집의 인도사람
카레 인사 건너 오고

아랫집은 중국말로
고추 기름 달달 볶네

어쩌나
오늘 저녁엔
담북장을 끓일 텐데


-2014년 1월 한나 프레스-

# Scent of neighbors

The Indian across the hall
Says hello with curry

The folks downstairs fry
Chili oil with Chinese words

So sorry
I will be cooking
*dambukjang tonight


*dambukjang: fast-fermented bean paste soup; has a strong pungent smell

Jatropha integerrima
Family Name:Euphorbiaceae

Plumeria rubra cultivars
Family Name:Apocynaceae

# 빨래를 개며

씻어 말린 빨래를
하늘에서 걷어와

이치에 맞게 접어
서랍장에 정리하네

마음도
곱게 접으면
정리하기 쉬워질까

# Folding laundry

I take down sun-dried
laundry from the sky

fold it in order
tuck away in drawers

Could hearts
be folded so neatly
to be so easily tucked away

Jatropha podagrica
Family Name:Euphobiaceae

국그릇

Dillenia suffruticosa
Family Name:Dilleniaceae

노을이
지붕 아래로 안겨 드는 저녁에는
식구들의 뱃속이 모두 다 빈 그릇
배추 된장국을 끓였다
수저 놓고 김치 담고 국자를 들고 보니
이가 빠진 국그릇 하나가
얼굴에 분을 바른 것처럼 꽃 그림은 여전한데
벌써 이렇게 나이가 들었구나
속 풀이 북어와 무 멸치를 우려낸 날과
저 태어난 날은 잊은 듯 지나가도
가족들 생일 따라 미역국을 끓인 날에도
한 그릇 담아 내던 사랑
틀니가 없으면
무 생채 한 가닥도 입에 넣지 못하는
늙으신 어머니처럼
국그릇에게도 이를 맞춰 줄 수 있을까
국을 담지 못해도 그냥 버릴 수가 없어서
깨끗한 물 한 가득 채우고 향초를 띄워준다
스스로는 빛도 내지 않는
나의 국그릇

# Soup bowl

Sunset

embraced under the evening rooftop

My family's stomachs are empty bowls

I cook cabbage doenjang* soup

After I set the spoons and serve the kimchi

and pick up the ladle

I see a chipped bowl

its flowery prints still blushing like an adorned face

yet when has it grown so old

Through days of simmering dried pollack for hangovers and

radish and anchovies

of cooking seaweed soup for every birthday in the family

even when its own birthday was forgotten like nothing

it was serving a bowlful of love

I wonder if I could fill its chips

as I do for my old mother

who cannot even put in her mouth

a strip of radish without dentures

Though no longer fit for soup I dare not throw it away
I fill it with clear water and float a scented candle
It doesn't even shine for itself
My dear soup bowl


*doenjang: fermented soybean paste

Solandra longiflora
Family Name:Solanaceae

Mussaenda 'Dona Eva'
Family Name:Rubiaceae

# 사춘기

어리던 화초 아이
꽃봉보리 내밀어요

가슴 속에 솟는 뿔도
개화기를 알리네요

선불리 꺾지 말아요
사랑해주면 꽃 펴요

# Puberty

Little plant child
pushes out its bud

Horn in its heart
says it's time to blossom

Don't be rash and break it
for love will make it bloom

Costus woodsonii
Family Name:Costaceae

늙은 오빠

Clerodendrum paniculatum
Family Name:Labiatae

오빠와 나는
어머니가 해주신 무 갈치 찜을
서로 발라 먹으려고 다투던 젓가락들
한 집에 산 날은 그리 길지 않았다
오빠는 장가가고 나는 시집오고
어머니는 지금도 그 자리에 남겨진
남매들의 빈 접시
어느 계절의 어느 모퉁이부터인지
오빠가 늙었다
오빠의 식구들을 주렁주렁 달아 놓고
오빠가 병이 들었다
가을 달빛이 차가워지는 밤
더 늙으신 어머니는
등이 굽은 신작로를 올라 가다
구절초 꽃 핀 마실 길을 지나치고
한평생 그림자가 되어
예배당으로 걸어 가신다.


-2014년 10월 한나 프레스-

# Old brother

My older brother and I
were chopsticks that fought for more
bits of mother's steamed cutlassfish and radish
The days we lived together were not so long
After he got married and so did I
mother still remains in our place
like our empty dishes
Around some corner of some season
brother became old
With an entire family hanging on to him
brother became ill
On a night when autumn moonlight grows cold
my mother even older than before
goes up the bent-back pavement road
avoids the chrysanthemum path where she used to picnic
and becomes an age-old shadow
walking to church.

Bauhinia kockiana
Family Name:Leguminosae

Antigonon leptopus
Family Name:Polygonaceae

# 소복한

저물 녘 밥상 앞에
소복하게 모여 앉아

소복한 웃음꽃을
식구 모두 피워가면

소복한 이야기 거리
그릇 마다 소복해

# Plentiful

Sitting around
the dinner table aplenty

All in the family
blossoming smiles aplenty

Plentiful stories
in every bowl aplenty

Buddleja davidii
Family Name:Buddlejaceae

Bougainvillea
Family Name:Nyctaginaceae

# 책

꽃잎의 책장을
한 장 한 장 넘기다 보면

찬비 내리는 세상에서도
환하게 필 수 있는

지혜가 가득합니다
한두 송이 읽다 보면

# Book

Turning page by page
the books of floral leaves

I learn to bloom and shine
in a world of cold and rain

Finding full of wisdom
every blossom that I read

Tabernaemontana divaricata
Family Name:Apocynaceae

# 여름나무의 단상

Couroupita guianensis
Family Name:Lecythidaceae

이 땅 적도에 사는 동안
한 계절에 머물러 서 있는
나는 여름 나무

잔가지 끝에 새잎이 돋아
말초신경이 봄을 맞으며 짜릿한데도
정글 속에 파묻힌 우리는
오늘도 여름나무

살아 있기에 빛이 바래는 날 있는 거지
붉고 노란 물 드는 일로 손끝부터 저린데
그렇게 온통 나이는 가지마다 가을인데
여름나무들은 광합성의 노동으로 숨이 가쁘다

우수수 하나도 남김없이
버려야 할 때는 모두 떨구어야지
언제 손에서 놓아야 하는지
계절을 잊어 때를 모른다
앙상한 가지로만 남아서
속을 다 드러내도 부끄럽지 않고
매서운 혹한도 견디는 겨울나무가 되어
한 계절쯤은 꼿꼿하게
살아내고 싶다

# Thoughts of a summer tree

While living here on the equator
I who stand fixed on one season
am a summer tree

Even when new leaves bud on small branch tips
peripheral nerves all fired up in anticipation of spring
we are buried deep in the jungle
still today a summer tree

Your colors can fade only when you're alive
Even with their fingertips numb from tinting red and yellow
even with every single branch pacing towards autumn
summer trees are short of breath by labor of photosynthesis

When it is time for letting go
everything should be shed without a trace
Having forgotten the seasons
we know not when to let it go
Remaining only as skinny branches

and unashamed of my exposed inside
I want to be a winter tree that
braves the harsh cold and steadfastly live
for at least a season

Thunbergia erecta
Family Name:Acanthaceae

Strobilanthes cusia
Family Name：Acanthaceae

# 당신

당신은 깊게 볼수록
꽃 손과 꽃 대궁을

어깨의 푸른 잎과
마음 깊은 뿌리까지

아직은 다 알 수 없는
하늘 나무 한 그루

# You

The more I watch your
flowery hands and flowery stalk

shoulders of green leaves
and thoughtful deep roots

A tree of the sky you are
still beyond my grasp

Musa coccinea
Family Name：Musaceae

# 배추 전

Pereskia belo
Family Name:Cactaceae

배추 전을 드셔 보셨나요
친정에서 어머니가 해주시던 음식인데요
배춧잎을 한 장씩 떼어서 씻고
밑동을 칼자루로 자근자근 찧어 누르고
밀가루 물을 흠뻑 적신 후에
기름 두른 프라이팬에 굽는 건데요
밑이 익었을 때 주걱으로 뒤집으면
배추나무 그림이 한 장 노릇하게 구워져 있어요
배춧잎의 잎맥 한 줄 한 줄이
나뭇가지 마냥 뻗어 있지요
배춧잎 하얀 줄기는 나무둥치이고요
나무 그늘 아래에는 한 사람
막걸리에 배추 전을 한 입 드시네요
밭일을 하시다가 새참 드시는 아버지
딸을 공부시켜 도회지로 시집 보내셨지요
나는 고층 아파트 먹구름 도시에 살면서도
배추 전을 부치다가 문득
고향마을 느티나무 한 그루 볼 수 있는
마음의 눈을 물려주고 가셨어요
배추 전을 부치는 일이
땅을 부치는 일보다 수월할 거라고
프라이팬 기름이 자작거리며 말해 주네요

# Cabbage jeon*

Have you tried cabbage jeon

My mother used to make it for me

You take apart the cabbage leaves, wash them one by one

squish the leaf bottom with the knife handle

soak it deep in watery flour

and cook on an oiled frying pan

If you turn it over with a spatula

when the bottom is well cooked

you will find a picture of a cabbage tree

baked in brownish yellow

Every vein of the cabbage leaf

runs like branches of a tree

The white stem of the cabbage leaf is the base of the tree trunk

and under the shade of the tree sits a man

tasting cabbage jeon with makgeolli**

My father taking a break from laboring in the fields

who sent his daughter to school and married her off to town

Even though I live in a high-rise in a gloomy city

he left me a heart that can

see the elm tree of my home town

in the cabbage jeon I cook

It would be easier to cook cabbage jeon

than to plow and till the fields

the frying pan tells me with its cackling oil


*jeon: a pancake-like food, cooked with vegetables, kimchi, etc.

**makgeolli: milky sweet alcoholic beverage typically made with rice

Barleria repens 'Orange Bugle'
Family Name: Acanthaceae

Paraserianthes falcataria
Family Name:Leguminosae

# 둥지

새들의 고운 목청 동네를 깨우자 마자
눈꺼풀 빗장 열고 달려 드는 아침 햇살
뚝배기 끓기도 전에 아기 울음 안아 주네

번갯불에 콩을 볶고 된장 찌개 아침 밥상
큰 아들 유치원 버스 등 떠밀어 보내고 나면
깃털 몇 흩날리는 새들의 아침 둥지

출근한 아비 새가 태양에게 날아가
노을 속에 모이 물고 돌아오는 서쪽하늘
어미 새는 한낮 빛살에 기저귀를 말렸네

펴고 날아야 할 날개가 있다면
날개 접고 머무는 사랑도 있어서
둥지는 나뭇가지에 얹혀서도 둥근 집

# Nest

As soon as the fair voice of the birds wakes the town
The morning sunshine rushes in unlatching the eyelids
It caresses the baby's cry even before the pot starts boiling

Breakfast with bean paste soup quickly thrown together
Push the first son onto the bus headed to kindergarten
Then only feathers remain flying in the birds' morning nest

Father bird off to work flies into the sun
returning from the westward sky
carrying seeds through the sunset
mother bird has dried the diapers in the sun's rays at noon

Just like wings need to spread and fly
love needs to fold its wings and stay
The nest is a round home even on the branch it hangs

Ruellia rosea
Familly Name:Acanthaceae

마늘, 꽃이 되다 부 Garlic becomes a flower

Dillenia philippinensis
Family Name:Dilleniaceae

# 꽃잎이 떨어지다

이 빠진 아이는
입 벌려 활짝 웃고

꽂잎 빠진 할머니는
입을 가리신다

마음에
꽃이 지는 일
손으로 숨기신다


-2014년 12월 한나프레스-

# A petal falls

Child with a lost tooth
smiles wide open

Grandmother with a lost petal
covers her mouth

Hiding
under her hand
her heart's withering flower

Belamcanda chinensis
Family Name:Iridaceae

Heliconia  rostrata
Family Name :Heliconiaceae

# 미안하다 도마뱀

고층까지 기어 오른
싱가포르 도마뱀

내 집 문서 들이대며
내쫓아도 버틴다

제 터에
차린 내 살림
지켜보는 눈초리

# Sorry, gecko

The Singaporean gecko
climbs up the high-rise

Doesn't budge even when
I wave the house deed at him

Still eyes
watching my home
settled upon his land

Pachystachys lutea
Family Name：Acanthaceae

Costus speciosus
Family Name:Costaceae

# 대구 찜

하루를 성실하게 산 사람들을 위하여
오늘은 대구 찜을 준비합니다
올곧게 자란 대파를 다듬고
그늘에서 자란 버섯도 올리고
한 겹을 빼앗겨도 속이 남아 있는 양파와
품어준 저 바다의 깊이와 넓이를 감사하는
대구 한 마리의 다소곳함
청 고추와 홍 고추의 사랑 이야기를 들으며
갖은 양념으로 함께 버무립니다
큰 쟁반에 콩나물 한 봉지를 쏟아놓고
뉴스를 들으며 하나씩 다듬습니다
이 칼칼한 대구 찜을 하는데
흙에도 짠 바다에도 발 한 번 넣지 않고
높은 틀에서 수경 재배된 콩나물
노랑 머리들은 어찌할까 고민을 하다가요
미련 없이 따버리기로 했습니다
하루를 땀 흘리며 성실하게 산 사람들의
평화로운 저녁을 위하여
대구 찜을 요리하며

# Daegu jjim*

For those who lived the day in earnest
today's dish is daegu jjim
I clean incorrigible green onions
put in mushrooms that grew in the shades
onions that stay full layer after layer
and the modesty of a codfish
grateful of the depth and width of the ocean's womb
I mix together all condiments
listening to the love story of red and green pepper
I spill open a bag of bean sprout on a large tray
and clean them one by one listening to the news
What to do with the yellow heads
that have laid foot neither on dirt nor salty sea
cultured with water safe upon a sieve
Would they be right for this zesty daegu jjim
I decide to boldly pick them off
Cooking daegu jjim
for a peaceful dinner of
those who've labored the day in earnest

*daegu jjim: a spicy dish of braised codfish and vegetables

Heliconia stricta
Family Name:Heliconiaceae

Lantana camara
Family Name:Verbenaceae

# 봄으로 가는 사천여행

낮은 땅 이슬비에 양귀비꽃 촉촉한데
높은 산 나뭇가지엔 얼음 꽃이 단단하다
이른 봄 맘 한구석에 남아 있는 겨울처럼

# Sichuan trip towards spring

Poppies are moist with dew on the lowlands
But branches on hilltops are hardened with flowery ice
Just as winter lingers in the corner of early spring's heart

Arundina species
Family Name:Orchidaceae

Musa rosacea
Family Name:Musaceae

# 귀한 것에 대한

흔하던 대두 콩나물
싱가포르엔 드물어

해 뜨는 새벽시장으로
눈 비비며 달려간다

이제야 귀한 줄 안다
먼데 있는
사람처럼

# On precious things

Soy sprouts were so common
But they're rare in Singapore

I run to the early market at dawn
Barely awake from sleep

Now I know how precious they are
Like those
Who are far away

Renanthera Kalsom
Family Name:Orchidaceae

Morinda citrifolia
Family Name:Rubiaceae

# 마늘, 꽃이 되다

빛 들지 않는 땅 속 마늘 송이 꽃 송이
곧게 솟은 꽃대 위 꽃자루에 피지 못해
꽃대는 마늘종으로 장독 안에 한 가득

마늘이 꽃 되었으니 여기저기 부름 받아
나물 무침 고기 반찬 탕 국에도 어우러져
아픔이 참 매웠으나 아픔들을 위로한다

자주 보면 사랑되는 것 사람 일만 아니구나
내 곁에 머물러 하고픈 말 많아서
마늘 향 손가락 끝에 오래도록 배어 있다


-제12회 동서문학상 맥심상 수상작-

# Garlic becomes a flower

A bulb of garlic, a bulb of flower, dark underground
Could not blossom on the flower stalk rising straight above
Its stem became maneuljong* filling the earthen crock

Garlic became a flower, called upon everywhere
Mingling with greens, garnishes, steaks, sides, stew, and soup
Though its pain was fiery now it comforts other pains

To see often is to love; not only is it true of humans
Staying by my side with so many words to tell
The scent of garlic lingers on my fingertips for so long


*maneuljong: spicy side dish made of garlic stems

Tristellateia australasiae
Family Name：Malpighiaceae

Ixora 'Super King'
Family Name:Rubiaceae

# 곤충학 숙제

그 모습 그대로
핀에 박힌 표본이 될래

날개가 찢어져도
날아오르는 나비 될래

아직도
다 풀지 못한
몇 십 년 된 이 숙제

# Entomology homework

Would you be a specimen
pinned the way you are

Or fly up like a butterfly
Even with torn wings?

Still
unfinished
decades-old homework

Costus malortieanus
Family Name:Costaceae

Neomarica gracilis
Family Name：Iridaceae

# 지는 날

꽃이 지는 날에는
바람이 날아와서

떨어지는 꽃잎 안고
흙 위에 뉘어준다

사람이 지는 날에도
바람이 부는구나

# Falling day

On the day when flowers fall
the wind flies in

embraces the falling petals
and lays them on the dirt

On the day when a person falls
so does the wind blow

Heliconia psittacorum 'Andromeda'
Family Name：Heliconiaceae

# 겨울을 여행하다

여름의 나라에서
별똥별처럼 밤 하늘을 날아
사뿐히 내린 고국은 겨울이다
살아있는 호흡들이
추운 세상을 입김으로 데우며
그랬었다 그림을 그린다

Hymenocallis speciosa
Family Name：Amaryllidaceae

고향 근방 오래된 감나무들이
까치 밥을 차려놓고 기다려도
자식들은 날개 달린 철새
새빨간 산수유가
파란 하늘을 바탕 삼고
차가운 눈밭 위에 매달려 있어도
아랑곳 하지 않는 사랑
그랬었다

여행의 반환점에 서 계시는
어머니를 향해 달려가는 길
길 없는 길을 걸어 흰 눈은 내리고
이마와 콧잔등 온 가슴으로 눈을 맞을 때
겨울의 말 한 마디 귓가에 날아든다
겨울을 떠나 살던 내가
그랬었다
겨울이었다고

-2013년 12월 한나 프레스-

# Traveling winter

Flying across the nighttime sky like a shooting star
from the land of summer
it is winter as I land smoothly in my home land
All breathing things
warming the cold world with puffs of breath
and so they were painting a picture

Though the old persimmon trees near home
save a few fruits for the birds and wait
children are migrating birds with wings
Blood red dogwood seeds
a love that does not mind
hanging above the cold snow fields
against the blue sky
and so it was

Running towards mother standing
at the turning point of my trip
Walking the pathless path as white snow falls
embracing the snow with my forehead and nose and all my heart

a word of the winter flies into my ear

I who lived away from winter

so it said

was winter

Pentas lanceolata
Family Name:Rubiaceae

Hibiscus rosa-sinensis cultivars
Family Name:Malvaceae

# 詩

잠 못 드는 밤에는

고드름 끝의 침 말고

차가운 발 끝부터

가슴까지 덮어주어

솜이불 포근해지는

시 한 편이 되고파

# Poem

On sleepless nights I'd rather not

pierce like the point of an icicle

but cover all the way from

the cold feet to the heart

like a warm cotton blanket

A poem I want to be

Pseuderanthemum carruthersii var. reticulatum
Family Name:Acanthaceae

Lantana montevidensis
Family Name:Verbenaceae

# 싱가포르 강가에서

추운 한국에는 온실이 있고
더운 싱가포르에는 냉실이 있다

어머니의 가슴 속에는
냉실 같은 자식이 머물고

자식들의 가슴 속에는
온실 같은 어머니가 흐르고

# By the Singapore river

In cold Korea there are greenhouses
And in hot Singapore there are air-conditioned domes

In mother's heart
Children linger like conditioned air

In the children's hearts
Mother like a greenhouse flows

Sanchezia speciosa
Family Name:Acanthaceae

사람소리 **part 4** 부 Human sounds

Kopsia fruticosa
Family Name:Apocynaceae

# 갓난 아기

갓 벗은 꼬투리에서
콩알 하나
태어났다

실 뿌리 발가락과
새싹 다섯 손가락

눈빛을 먹고 자라는
우주 안의
사랑아

-2014년 샘터 6월호-

# A newborn

A pea
is born
from a freshly shed pod

Toes of fibrous roots
and five fingers of buds

Love
of the universe
feeding on my gaze

Complaya trilobata
Family Name:Compositae

Rhodomyrtus tomentosa
Family Name:Myrtaceae

# 옆에 앉다

퇴근한 당신의 밤
바깥일을 잠 재우려고
보지도 않는 TV앞에
말 없이 앉아 계시네
어두운 당신 옆으로
나도 가만 앉았네

# Sitting next to you

Late night back from work
to put to sleep the busy day
you sit silently in front of
the TV you're not watching
next to the gloomy you
I sit quietly too

Centratherum punctatum
Family Name:Compositae

# 닭 너는

더운 바람에도 오싹해지는 속을 챙길까 하여
삼계탕 앞에 앉아 있다 닭은 죽고
나는 사는 것인가
뚝배기 안에 담긴 닭은
닭 똥 같은 눈물을 흘릴 시간
얼마나 있었을까
세상에서는 머리의 붉은 볏으로 호통 치던

Whitfieldia elongata
Family Name : Acanthaceae

닭울녘의 목청이 뽀얀 국물에 녹아있다
닭의 살을 내 살에 붙일수록
하나씩 드러나는 뼈 조각들
긴 목뼈 잔잔하게 이어져 눈 뜬 밤처럼 길고
눕혀도 솟아나는 날개 뼈는
하늘을 저어도 제자리인데
먹이를 찾던 발가락과 발목까지 다 버리고
그 붉은 벼슬을 스스로 내려놓을 수 있었다면
갈비뼈 둥글게 마음을 지킬 수 있었다면
거룩하기조차 한 삼계탕
온 몸을 내주고
죽은듯하면서도 살아서 말하는 닭의 심지가
반 접시 뼈로만 남아도 미소는 단단하다
사는 것은 내 안의 속을 다 비우고
인삼 대추 마늘로 나의 살 냄새마저 지워 버리고
하얀 찹쌀로 미련처럼 공허한 속을 채워 넣은 후
한 끼 밥보다 든든한 약이 되는 것이구나
그래서 닭 너는
높이 날지 않았어도
내 안에서 깊게 나는 새가 된다

-2012년 10월 한나프레스-

# You, dear chicken

To strengthen my bones that shiver even in hot wind
I sit in front of a bowl of samgyetang*; does the chicken die
to make me live
Would the chicken inside the hot pot
have had time to shed the tears
like chicken droppings
The throat that hollered at the world with the
red comb on its head now melts in milky broth
Bones reveal themselves one by one
as I attach its skin onto mine
The long neck bone calmly goes on like a long sleepless night
and wing bones that keep stretching up
flail at the sky to no avail
Yet if it threw away its toes and ankles that sought for food
willingly let down its red comb
and kept its faith inside its round ribs
how holy is this samgyetang
Giving its whole body
dying yet living, the chicken's will speaks
its smile still resolute even when reduced to a half dish of bones
To live is to empty myself, I learn

to erase the scent of my flesh with ginseng, jujube and garlic

to fill my clingy inner hollow with white sticky rice

and then to become a potent tonic better than a meal of rice

Thus you, dear chicken

even though you did not fly high

you become a bird that flies deep inside of me


*samgyetang: chicken soup cooked by filling the chicken with ginseng, jujube, sticky rice, and various spices, usually eaten on hot days to boost one's energy

Hibiscus rosa-sinensis cultivars
Family Name:Malvaceae

Plumbago auriculata
Family Name:Plumbaginaceae

# 사람 소리

자식이 떠나고 세월도 떠난 집에
노을처럼 누워있는 부모님의 전화기
'고객님 안녕하십니까' 그 소리도 반가운

# Human sounds

In a house where children and time have left
My parents' handphone lies like the sunset
Even 'may I speak with the head of the household'
sounds welcome

Carphalea kirondron
Family Name:Rubiaceae

Petrea volubilis
Family Name:Verbenaceae

# 보금자리

당신은 졸린 내 등
토닥토닥 안고서

까만 창 달빛 들여
어둔 마음 밝히시네

가쁜 숨 가라앉히고
지친 하루 눕는 자리

# Nesting place

You caress with a pat
my sleepy back

Let the moonlight in through black windows
to brighten my gloomy heart

A place to catch my breath
and lay down my tired day

Tarenna odorata
Family Name:Rubiaceae

Adenium obesum
Family Name：Apocynaceae

# 호박이 웃다

지난 봄 붕붕 날아든 꿀벌을 따라서
어머니의 젖 떼고 시집을 온 후에는
아무리 꽃을 피워도 호박꽃만 만발하네

꽃송이 아랫배가 봉긋해진 여름날
장미가 되고 싶어 가시를 돋우니
호박 잎 손바닥 위엔 솜 가시만 보송보송

새콤한 가을햇살 입덧 속을 잠 재우고
가슴 안에 조롱조롱 잉태된 씨앗들로
궁둥이 펑퍼짐해도 내 웃음은 황금빛

# A pumpkin smiles

Since I followed the bumblebee that buzzed in last spring
and left my mother's breasts to get married away from home
All I could blossom were a bunch of pumpkin flowers

One summer day as my flowering underbelly started to bulge
I wished to be a rose and pushed out my thorns
but all I got was prickly hair on my green leafy palms

Sour sweet rays of autumn sun quell the morning sickness
As my heart gets pregnant with all the teeming seeds
My buttocks may be flabby yet my smile is golden

Zephyranthes candida
Family Name: Amaryllidaceae

Costus lucanusianus
Family Name:Costaceae

# 꽃잎, 꽃 입

소문을 가득 품은
꽃 입에 귀 기울이다

꽃은 말을 참기보다
하기가 힘에 겨워

앙다문 꽃잎의 곁을
소리 없이 지나간다


-2013년 7월 한나 프레스-

# Floral leaves, floral lips

I listen carefully to floral lips
holding mouthful of rumors

Flowers find it harder to
speak words than to keep

So silently I pass by
tightly sealed floral leaves

Crossandra infundibuliformis
Family Name：Acanthaceae

Thalia geniculata
Family Name:Marantaceae

# 자투리

가을이 입다가 버리고 간 옷과
아이들을 좇아서 자라지 못한 옷
오늘은 집 안에서 자투리가 되었다

한 세상 돌리는 재봉틀에 물려서
박음질로 걸어온 길 구불구불 하구나
인생길 숙련되게 곧은 길 박지 못했다

가위로 잘라놓은 작금의 자투리들
생각하는 무늬가 유연하지 못하여
시대의 흐름조차 탈 수 없는 촌스러움

그래도 한두 조각 자투리 천 잇다 보니
백화점에 진열된 유명 상품 아니어도
물김치 잘 익은 밥상 식탁보는 되겠다

-2014년 3월 한나 프레스-

# Scrap

Clothes that last autumn left behind
Clothes that could not grow up with the children
Today they became scraps of cloth lying around the house

Caught in the sewing machine of spinning life
I see that I walked such a crooked backstitched path
Never could my life's walk be a stitch so skillfully straight

These fresh scraps all cut up by scissors
Their patterns of thought lack flexibility
A dowdiness unfit for riding the trends of time

When these scraps are put together one by one
They're no brand item showing in department stores
But at least they make a tablecloth
for a nice watery kimchi dinner

Angelonia biflora
Family Name:Scrophulariaceae

Thunbergia laurifolia
Family Name:Acanthaceae

# 세월 따라 가는 사람

나뭇잎 물이 들고 세월이 흘러 가네
세월이 흘러가니 물드는 맘 아쉬워라
흐르는 세월을 따라 사람도 흘러 가니

낙엽이 떨어지고 세월이 떠나 가네
세월이 떠나가니 비는 맘 채워질까
떠나는 세월을 따라 사람도 떠나 가니

사람이 흐르고 세월이 떠나갈 때
떨어진 낙엽 위에 넋을 놓고 슬퍼하네
세월에 정 깊은 사람 그 세월과 함께 가니

# People flow along with time

Leaves turn red and time flows along
The flow of time makes a wistful heart turn red
As people flow along with the flow of time

Leaves fall down and time flows away
Will the leaving of time fill my empty heart
As people leave along with the leaving of time

When people flow and time leaves
I achingly grieve over fallen leaves
As people of my loving times leave as that time goes by

Orthosiphon aristatus
Family Name:Labiatae

Erythrina fusca
Family Name:Leguminosae

# 피아노

한 집안에 산다 하여
음악이 흐르진 않아

희고 검은 그 기분을
높고 낮은 그 속내를

내 손이
배우고 익혀
안마해 줘야 노래하네

# Piano

Living as a household
doesn't make music flow

The feelings black and white
the thoughts high and low

My hands must learn and master
the massaging touch that makes him sing

Mussaenda 'Dona Luz'
Family Name:Rubiaceae

Catharanthus roseus
Family Name:Apocynaceae

# 섬나라에서

적도의 바다 위에
나 홀로 떠 있는 섬

문을 열고 기다리다
마음이 저무는 날

그 사람 오지를 않아
또 하루가 어둡다

# On an island

I am a lonely island
floating on a tropic sea

A day of waiting by the door
till dusk fills the heart

Another gloomy day
as he does not come

Calathea crotalifera
Family Name:Marantaceae

Calathea loeseneri
Family Name：Marantaceae

# 오래

귀가 깊은 꽃들을
오래 보고 있노라면

꽃도 나를 오래 보아
내 속을 다 털어 놓네

듣는 귀 향기로워서
참말로만 고하네

# Long

When I stare long at
Flowers with deep ears

They stare back at me long
So I pour out my heart

The ears listen so fragrantly
I can only tell the truth

Russelia equisetiformis
Family Name:Scrophulariaceae

# 다른 길로 가다 보면 다른 꽃이 보인다.

싱가포르에서 꽃을 만날 때는 눈보다 귀가 기울여졌습니다. 송이 마다 다른 이야기를 들려 주는데 사람들도 그렇지 않냐는 질문에 할 말을 잃은 적이 있습니다. 우리는 비슷한 것을 추구하고 사는 경우가 많기 때문입니다. 같은 목적지에 도달하지 않으면 불안하고 낙오자처럼 지내기도 합니다. 개개인의 가슴 속에 있는 유전자를 제대로 발현시킨다면 꽃이 된다는 것을 이들은 얘기해 주었습니다.

긴 시간 천천히 준비하고도 부족한 곳이 많지만 도와 주신 분들 덕분에 타국에서나마 책을 엮을 수가 있었습니다. 정성을 다하여 번역 해주신 박성열 교수님, 열대 꽃과 글의 집을 지어주신 디자이너 이호형 작

가님, 타국에서 한글의 공간을 마련해 주신 한나 프레스 이건기 편집장님 또한 시작부터 마칠 때까지 격려해 주고 기다려 주신 생각나눔 이기성 편집장님 감사합니다.

친정 아버지는 앉은뱅이 책상에서 평생 일기를 쓰셨습니다. 그리고 등으로 보여주신 글쓰기를 유산으로 물려주고 떠나셨습니다. 사랑의 후원자 남편과 두 아들 부모님들 그리고 이렇게 많은 꽃들을 창조하고 영감을 주시는 하늘의 아버지께 진심으로 감사를 드립니다.

인생을 걷다 보면 낯선 곳에 머물기도 하고 어려운 일을 겪기도 하고 예상치 못한 슬픔에 힘겨울 때가 많습니다. 왜 이러나 싶었지만 고개를 살짝 들고 보니 다른 길에는 다른 꽃이 핀다는 것을 알았습니다. 어느 길에서든지 여러분 모두 행복하시길 바랍니다.

2015년 싱가포르 Bukit Batok에서
금혜정